I Can Do It!

by Tracey Corderoy

Illustrated by

Caroline Pedler

tiger tales

Baby Bear had a new backpack.
It was *wonderful*, but the big green
button was tricky for little paws!
All morning, Baby Bear tried
and tried to open and close it.

"Mommy! Look!"
he cried at last.

"I can do it!"

"Great job!" Mommy said. "Why don't we put some books in to take back to the library?"

"I can do it!" Baby Bear smiled. And he squeezed *all* the books into his backpack. Every one!

But it was just a
little too heavy…

Oops!

Mommy took a few books out to carry and then tried to help Baby Bear with his coat.

"No, I can do it!" Baby Bear said.

He wriggled into it and buttoned *all* the buttons!

"Come on,
Bailey," he said
to his toy bunny.
"Let's go!"

Baby Bear skipped into town
and stopped at the crosswalk.
"I can press the button!"
he said.
But somebody *else*
pressed it first....

"I wanted to do it!" Baby Bear grumbled.

And he went on sadly with Mommy.

At the library, Baby Bear raced off to find Bailey's favorite bunny book. But it was up **very** high.

"Don't worry, Bailey," Baby Bear said. "I'll get it!"

He stood on tiptoe, but he couldn't reach.
He hopped and he jumped, but he *still*
couldn't reach.

"Rats!" said Baby Bear.
He really wanted to get the
book *all by himself.*

So Baby Bear built a big tower of cushions
and clambered right to the top.
But suddenly, the tower
started to sway ....

Wibble!

Wobble!

"Oh, no!" cried Baby Bear. And down he tumbled …

...bump!

"Mommy!" he howled, and
Mommy rushed over.

"Oh, Baby Bear!" she said. "You must be careful."

"I couldn't reach the book," sniffed Baby Bear.

Mommy gave him a big hug. "You can do *lots* of things by yourself. But when things are too tricky, you just need to ask for help."

"Okay," Baby Bear nodded.

Mommy took the book off the shelf.
Baby Bear and Bailey turned the
pages, and Mommy read the words.
Sometimes having a little bit
of help was fine.

When it was time to go, Baby Bear packed his backpack and helped Mommy with her coat.

"I can do it!" Baby Bear said.

"Thank you, Baby Bear!"
smiled Mommy.
Then Baby Bear skipped
off home, singing...

"I can do it! Look at me.
I'm as clever as can be!
But when things are hard to do,
You are there to help me, too.
Now I clap my hands and say…
I can do it! Hip, hip, hooray!"

For Isaac, may learning that *you can do it* be great fun! x ~ T.C.

"If you can dream it, you can do it."—*Walt Disney* ~ C.P.

tiger tales

5 River Road, Suite 128, Wilton, CT 06897

Published in the United States 2014

Originally published in Great Britain 2014

by Little Tiger Press

Text copyright © 2014 Tracey Corderoy

Illustrations copyright © 2014 Caroline Pedler

ISBN-13: 978-1-58925-153-3

ISBN-10: 1-58925-153-9

Printed in China

LTP/1800/0750/0913

10 9 8 7 6 5 4 3 2 1

For more insight and activities, visit us at www.tigertalesbooks.com